HAPPY HONEY

THE BEST
FALL OF ALL

HAPPY HONEY

THE BEST
FALL OF ALL

written by Laura Godwin
pictures by Jane Chapman

MARGARET K. McELDERRY BOOKS
NEW YORK · LONDON · TORONTO · SYDNEY · SINGAPORE

For the children at the Marigold
School in Victoria, B.C.
—L. G.

For Olivia and Georgie
—J. C.

Margaret K. McElderry Books
An imprint of Simon & Schuster Children's Publishing Division
1230 Avenue of the Americas, New York, NY 10020

Book design by Sonia Chaghatzbanian
The text of this book is set in Century Schoolbook.
The illustrations are rendered in acrylic.
Printed in the United States of America

2 4 6 8 10 9 7 5 3 1

Library of Congress Cataloging-in-Publication Data
Godwin, Laura.
The best fall of all / written by Laura Godwin ; pictures by Jane Chapman.
p. cm. — (Happy Honey ; 3)
Summary: Happy the dog and Honey the cat enjoy playing outside on a fall day.
ISBN 0-689-84713-0
[1. Dogs—Fiction. 2. Cats—Fiction. 3. Autumn—Fiction.]
I. Chapman, Jane, ill. II. Title.
PZ7.G5438 Be 2002
[E]—dc21
2001044120

FIRST
EDITION

Fall is here.

Happy is happy.

Happy likes fall.

Woof, woof.

Happy goes out.

Meow, meow.

Honey goes out.

Honey likes fall too.

Honey sees birds.

She sees
apples and pumpkins.

She sees fall leaves.
She sees fall leaves fall.

Meow, meow.

Honey feels the wind.

The wind is cold.

Honey does not like
the wind.

Woof, woof.

Here comes Happy.

Happy is warm.

Happy likes the wind.

Happy will help Honey
get warm too.

Woof, woof.

Happy runs.

Meow, meow.

Honey runs too.

Happy and Honey
run fast.

They run fast
past the birds.
They run fast
past the pumpkins.

They run fast and
FALL
into the leaves.

What fun!

Then Happy and Honey
run home.

Woof, woof.

Meow, meow.

Happy and Honey

go in.

Now Honey is warm
and happy.
Like Happy.

And Happy is warm
and happy.
Like Honey.

Happy and Honey
fall asleep.

This is the best
fall of all.